# Return of the
# Locomotive Driver

Abdolhai Shammasi

**TSL Drama**

First published in Great Britain in 2025
By TSL Publications, Rickmansworth

Copyright © 2025 Abdolhai Shammasi

ISBN: 978-1-917426-21-3

Cover courtesy of :
Raha Ghanbari

# Characters

LOCOMOTIVE DRIVER [LD] - early sixties
OLD MAN [OM]
NEIGHBOR
OLD NEIGHBOR [OLD N]
VOICE of WOMAN
VOICE of CHILD

# Running Time

50 minutes

The stage is a blind alley with some houses. The windows are covered with thick curtains so that the inside light does not show from the windows at all. Only one house is seen on the left side of the stage with dark windows. Before the stage right, there's a gate in front of which the railway track runs ahead giving the appearance of intersecting in two different places. Some metal scraps, a wheel and a crushed cabin are seen next to the railway track.

The LOCOMOTIVE DRIVER, in his early sixties, enters with a suitcase in his hand and stops after taking a few steps.

LD:    It was over, no matter what is was. I'd better stop talking to myself. The neighbors know me. [*Looks around cautiously.*] I wonder if there's someone after me. I think I've gone mad! [*Laughs coolly.*] No, not even a dog stays out of its home now late at night, let alone a human.

[*Stands next to the gate.*] What am I then? What am I...? I'm not a dog, I'm a human who has stayed out for the sake of them.

[*Pauses a second and then hits strongly the back of his hand on his forehead.*] A...h! I'm talking to myself again. I'm not crazy at all. I'd better behave myself.

[*Turns back and looks at the dark windows of the building.*] The children must be asleep now. They'll belong to me from tomorrow on. I'll talk to them about my travels. I won't have to hear that damned sound in my ears anymore.

[*Takes a cigarette out of his pocket, lights it, and begins walking home. But he slips and falls suddenly and heavily to the ground.*] Ouch...! Ouch...! My back! [*Points to somewhere above his head and begins shouting.*] Damn you all. Why don't you plow the snow from the path in front of your houses?

[*Gets off the ground with difficulty, puts on his hat, and picks up his suitcase dropped some meters away. One of the window curtains is pulled aside and the face of an* OLD MAN *appears, cool and pale.*

*The* LOCOMOTIVE DRIVER *turns back and goes a few steps away, horrified.*

*The same* OLD MAN *appears at another window again.*] No...! [*Covers his eyes with his hands.*] No...! It was just an illusion. [*Looks at the windows. The* OLD MAN *appears at the window of another house.*] Impossible...! [*This time walks to the house's door without looking at any windows but suddenly a heavy pile of snow drops before him from the rooftop of a building. The* LOCOMOTIVE DRIVER *steps back, horrified.*] Hey man! Look down first. You were about to drop it on my head.

NEIGHBOR: [*Looks down.*] Sorry, sir. It didn't hurt you, did it?

LD: Sheer nonsense!...

NEIGHBOR: It's dark out there. I failed to notice you.

LD: How come? How did you fail to notice me?

NEIGHBOR: I've already begged your pardon. I didn't expect to see anybody in the alley late at night.

LD: Do you mean I'm a dog then?

NEIGHBOR: Far from you, sir. You took me wrong.

LD: How come?... Ha...?

NEIGHBOR: Golly, I ate humble pie. Do you let me get down to my business?

LD: I had got nothing to do with you. I was just going on my way that you might drop a pile of snow on my head.

NEIGHBOR: I begged your pardon too.

LD: I'm talking about something else.

NEIGHBOR: What?

LD: Look at there. The next-door neighbor hasn't plowed the snow from the path before his house and I fell heavily to the ground.

NEIGHBOR: There must be something wrong with your shoes' tread.

LD: No, quite the opposite!

NEIGHBOR: Well, you must have fallen because you aren't well familiar with the alley.

LD: How come? I've been living here all my life. Now I'm going home too.

NEIGHBOR: Where?

LD: Home... My own house.

NEIGHBOR: Where is it? This is a blind alley. You must have come the wrong way.

LD: Not at all. I'm sure about it.

NEIGHBOR: I must know you if you're living in this neighborhood. Wait a minute. Let me come down there.

LD: [*To himself.*] It might have been dark that he couldn't recognize me. Yeah... He still doesn't know who I am. He will be happy when he recognizes me.

[*The* NEIGHBOR *comes down with a snowplow in his hand.*]

NEIGHBOR: [*Approaches the* LOCOMOTIVE DRIVER *and stares at him.*] No... I don't know you at all.

LD: How come?

NEIGHBOR: [*Starts plowing.*] Well, I don't know you.

LD: Look at me again. Maybe... you didn't look carefully.

NEIGHBOR: Never, sir. It's impossible for me to see anybody and forget his face.

LD: My house is somewhere in this alley... Look, the same building with all its lights off.

NEIGHBOR: [*Stares at the ground and plows the snow.*] I know all the inhabitants of this neighborhood.

LD: How come you don't know me then?

NEIGHBOR: Because I haven't seen you so far.

LD: Impossible! I'm living in that building.

NEIGHBOR: [*Raises his head.*] Which one?

LD: The same with a brown door.

NEIGHBOR: Do you mean that wooden door?

LD: Right... That's it.

NEIGHBOR: [*Approaches the mentioned building.*] Do you mean this one?

LD: Ok. It's mine.

NEIGHBOR: [*To himself.*] Impossible!

LD: Did you see I was right?

NEIGHBOR: [*To himself.*] He must have gone mad!

LD: Well, now say that you know me... please.

NEIGHBOR: Get down to your business, man. Don't put words in my mouth. It's about 25 solid years that I've been living here. This is an abandoned house. Its door has always been locked.

LD: I'm telling the truth. Why don't you believe me? I... I have two sons. One of them is a final-year student at university. The other one is still a high school student.

NEIGHBOR: [*Sneeringly.*] Well, what about your other highborn children? Do you have any other children as well?

LD: The other one...? Yeah, I have a daughter as well. Yeah... She's a student. A few days ago, someone came to propose marriage to her. He's a good young man... Well, I can't expect too much from someone

who is going to build a new life. Honor is essential...
Yeah, honor matters most.

NEIGHBOR: Right... honor is essential but that house has no owner anymore. May God bless his soul.

LD: May God bless the soul of all the dead ones. Who's dead?

NEIGHBOR: The owner of that house.

LD: The owner of that house is still alive... It's me.

NEIGHBOR: What's your job?

LD: I'm jobless right now. They took away my train.

NEIGHBOR: Who did so?

LD: The Railway Company. Because it's broken up. I've been the driver of that train for a long time. I've received a lot of Certificates of Appreciation. Some of them are here with me inside my suitcase. Would you like to have a look at them?

NEIGHBOR: No, I'm not in the mood for it.

[*Silence prevails for a while and the* NEIGHBOR *stares at the* LOCOMOTIVE DRIVER *reflectively.*]

LD: Did you say you knew me then?

NEIGHBOR: Yeah.... I've remembered.

LD: I knew... I knew...

NEIGHBOR: Right.... The owner of that house also used to be a train driver... How strange!

LD: Well, it's me...

NEIGHBOR: Impossible!... He must already be dead. All know about it.

LD: Do you mean I'm dead?

NEIGHBOR: I didn't witness it because we hadn't yet moved to this neighborhood. But it's said the owner of that house, who used to be a train driver, left home one day and never returned. That's why they thought he's dead.

LD: Please… please don't say that he's dead… He's still alive. It's me. Look… I'm still breathing. You can now see my breath. That house is mine too. Here is the key to its door. Would you like me to open it in your presence?

NEIGHBOR: But cobwebs have filled all over its door. The door hinges are covered with rust. I don't think you can open it.

LD: I opened it a few days ago and went in to my family.

NEIGHBOR: [*Stops working and starts doing some neck flexion exercises.*] It's about to finish.

LD: Look, that side-window is of my elder son's room.

NEIGHBOR: None of my business at all, man. Don't you see that I have to plow all the snow over there?

LD: What the hell is it?… Look… some snow was left here. It will be frozen till morning.

NEIGHBOR: Get down to your business, man.

LD: What do you have to do with me?

NEIGHBOR: Nothing. It's you that don't get off my back.

LD: I don't have anything to do with you.

NEIGHBOR: You do. It's an hour you're putting me on.

LD: I haven't put you on. I just talked to you.

NEIGHBOR: [*Shouting.*] What? I couldn't make head or tail of your words at all.

LD: Why are you shouting? [*Short pause.*] Stop shouting. My children are asleep. I don't want to bother you at all. I leave… I leave, bye… Go about your business.

NEIGHBOR: But you don't let me…

[*The* LOCOMOTIVE DRIVER *takes a few steps toward his house and stops. Turns around and looks behind hesitatingly.*]

LD: But he doesn't yet believe that I'm living here in this

house. I must prove that here is my home... [*Again, goes toward the* NEIGHBOR *and stops.*]

NEIGHBOR: What's happened? You wanted to go home, didn't you?

LD: Sorry... I didn't want to bother you. May I help you?

NEIGHBOR: No. Go plow the snow from the rooftop of your own house.

LD: Well, you believe I'm living in that house, don't you?

NEIGHBOR: It doesn't make any difference.

LD: Doesn't it even make a difference that I'm a locomotive driver?

NEIGHBOR: No, nobody has a job anyway... Move back a bit... Ah, damn it. I searched everywhere but I failed to find it.

LD: What are you talking about?

NEIGHBOR: A bigger snowplow.

LD: I have one. Would you like me to fetch it from my house?

NEIGHBOR: [*Sneeringly.*] From that house?!

LD: Yes...

NEIGHBOR: No need. Keep it for yourself.

LD: But it's a good one.

NEIGHBOR: I know. But it must have been decayed after such a long time.

LD: I've already bought it. Wait a moment. I'll fetch it for you.

[*The* LOCOMOTIVE DRIVER *goes toward his house hastily and enters. After plowing the snow for a while, the* NEIGHBOR *stops and moves his hands to warm up. The voice of a child is heard from inside the house.*]

VOICE of CHILD: Hasn't it finished yet, dad?

NEIGHBOR: It has, dear. I'm coming. It's cold outside. Stay inside...

[*The* NEIGHBOR *enters his house and locks the door behind himself. A few seconds later, the* LOCO-MOTIVE DRIVER *comes out of the house with a worn-out broken snowplow in his hand, agitated and confused. When he sees nobody is in the alley, he is glued to the spot and takes a few steps forward desperately and shakily.*]

LD: Nobody is here...! As if there has never been anybody either... [*Moves back and stands next to the house.*] Nobody was there inside the house either... Everything is covered in dust... as if one century has passed! But... but everything was in the right place when I came in a few days ago. But now...! No... no, I must have thought that I saw it. Nothing has now changed... How come all these events happened just within a few days?... Yeah... I thought I saw it. I have to go home like the others. Why should I stay out in such a cold weather? [*Picks up his suitcase and goes before his house. Stops for a while and then enters.*]

[*The* OLD MAN, *whose face appeared at the windows, enters the stage in worn-out and outsized clothes and carrying a pack on his shoulder, agitatedly and hastily like famine-stricken people. He holds a large loaf of bread in his hand from which he's eating greedily. He goes toward the house and takes a look inside cautiously. A few seconds later, he hides hastily behind a wall. The* LOCOMOTIVE DRIVER *comes out of the house with a scary laugh on his face.*]

LD: I've returned... I've come back home for ever... [*With a lump in his throat.*] I'm not supposed to go away anymore... I'm at home now...

[*The* LOCOMOTIVE DRIVER *takes a few steps away from the house and sits on the ground. The* OLD MAN *quietly throws himself into the house with a big morsel of bread in his hand.*]

LD:     Look! I've brought some souvenirs for you. Look! [*Puts his suitcase before himself and opens it.*] Here you are... I've brought this shirt for you... Go and try it on. It must fit you perfectly. [*Turns toward an imaginary person.*] It's for you! Be patient... I might not have forgotten you, might I?... Come on... Here you are. I've brought this pair of gloves for you, in the same color you liked. It's totally made of wool... Take it... I've brought all of them for you... No... This one is for your sister... Put it back... I've brought a pair of pants for you... Wait... It must be in the bottom of the suitcase... Aha, I've found it... I know it fits you perfectly... This is for... Well, that girl... She's going to marry... I should have brought many more things for her... This one is completely for your mother... Let me... let me wake her up too... I knew... I knew you'd be happy... [*Enters the house.*]

[*Silence prevails for a few seconds and then the terrible shout of the* LOCOMOTIVE DRIVER *is heard from inside the house. Then the* LOCO-MOTIVE DRIVER *runs away from inside the house and sprawls on the ground.*]

OM:     [*Off-stage.*] Get out of here... get out... Who are you?

LD:     Who are you then?... It's my house. Come out.

[*The* OLD MAN *appears within the door framework still with a piece of bread in his hand.*]

OM:     Here is my home... What do you want here?

LD:     What do I want here?!

OM:     I'll set fire to you if you step in my house again.

LD:     To me?!... In my own house?

OM:     House... Which house are you talking about? Here is my house. It's a long time I've been living here. Do you think you can kick me out of my own house? That's wishful thinking! [*Goes into the house and locks the door behind himself.*]

LD:     [*Gets up and starts knocking on the house door.*] You're lying... This is my house... Come out...

OM:     [*Off-stage.*] I don't... Here is my house.

LD:     My family lives in that house. All in this neighborhood know about it. [*Turns toward the windows of the houses around and begins shouting.*] Hey! I'm talking to all of you... Why have you closed your windows?... Why does nobody answer me? I've come back to my house... but... but a stranger doesn't let me in... [*Turns toward the house door.*] I'm telling you to come out.

OM:     [*Off-stage, with his mouth full.*] I won't... go somewhere else... where have you've been this time?

LD:     I belong here. [*To himself.*] Nobody is here to help me either... [*Shouting.*] Hey! At least, pull aside your curtains and let the valley lighten a bit. Hey, I'm talking to you... If I kept on driving the train from dawn to dusk, it was just for the sake of you... Now I've returned to my home.

    [*One of the windows opens and an* OLD NEIGHBOR *pokes his head out.*]

OLD N:     Hey, man. Who are you talking to? Have you lost your way?

LD:     I...I'm sorry... I...

OLD N:     Go home, dear. Why are you bothering the neighbors?

LD:     I've bothered nobody. I've just returned home. But... but a stranger has settled down in my house and doesn't let me in.

OLD N:     Why, dear?

| | |
|---|---|
| LD: | I don't know… |
| OLD N: | Which house do you mean? |
| LD: | The next-door house… Here is my home… You must know me… and my children as well… I'm your neighbor. |
| OLD N: | But nobody lives in that house, man. |
| LD: | We are… We're living there. |
| OLD N: | No, golly. That house has been ruined. |
| LD: | You're wrong, sir. |
| OLD N: | Not at all, man… Nobody can live in it. |
| LD: | How come?… We've been living in this house for more than 30 years. |
| OLD N: | [*Stares at the* LOCOMOTIVE DRIVER *hesitatingly.*] Golly, dear… It's late and cold. |
| LD: | I've already told you that… a stranger won't let me in my house… |
| OLD N: | Well man, go and file a complaint against him. |
| LD: | Where shall I go? |
| OLD N: | Wherever you wish, dear. |
| VOICE of OLD WOMAN: | [*From inside the house.*] Close the window. It's getting cold inside the room. Who are you talking to? |
| OLD N: | Leave here now, man. You will get cold. |
| LD: | What shall I do with that stranger then? |
| OLD N: | What you wish, man. |
| LD: | Do you think I'm lying? |
| OLD N: | No, dear… Go now. Your family is surely waiting for you. Take care of yourself. The ground has frozen. Watch your steps. |
| LD: | But he doesn't let me in… He… |
| | [*The* OLD NEIGHBOR *closes the window and pulls the curtain. The* LOCOMOTIVE DRIVER *is glued to the spot.*] |

| | |
|---|---|
| LD: | He doesn't let me in… [*Makes a sudden rush toward the house's door.*] Who do you think you are? Come out of my house… |
| OM: | [*Off-stage.*] What's going on there…? Why don't you let me calm down at all? Leave me alone. |
| LD: | I've got nothing to do with you. It's you who has settled down in my house and don't come out. |
| OM: | [*Off-stage.*] I've been living here for a long time. I know that I'll have no place to live if I leave here. Get down to your business… I'm tired. |
| LD: | [*Desperately.*] Come out…, please… Why does everything look somehow different? Everybody treats me like a stranger. But… but I shouldn't care about it. Now I have two young sons and a daughter of marriage-age. They… they certainly know their father well. Now I go and tell them how the neighbors treated me badly. [*Goes and stands at the house door.*] But… but first of all, I should kick him out of my house. |
| OM: | [*Off-stage.*] I will never let you kick me out of my house. |
| LD: | Again he called it his house. |
| OM: | [*Off-stage.*] Would you really like to come into the house too? |
| LD: | Obvious enough…! Why have I come a long way to here then? |
| OM: | [*Off-stage.*] All inside the house has been ruined and everything is covered in dust. |
| LD: | What about the home furniture? |
| OM: | [*Off-stage.*] Wait a minute… But there's nothing here. |
| LD: | How come? I was there last week. |
| OM: | [*Off-stage.*] Nothing is here… Or they've all been buried under dust. |

| | |
|---|---|
| LD: | Dust?! |
| OM: | [*Off-stage.*] It doesn't look like a house at all. It isn't worth living in anymore. Go somewhere else. |
| LD: | Well, what about my family? |
| OM: | [*Off-stage.*] Nobody is living here. |
| LD: | Look carefully. |
| OM: | [*Off-stage.*] I've already searched all the rooms but I've found nothing in them. Don't waste your time... Leave here. |
| LD: | What about that... side room... I mean that sun-facing room? |
| OM: | [*Off-stage.*] It's been left vacant for many years... No sign of life is seen here. |
| LD: | You're lying. By speaking this nonsense, you want to stop me entering my own house. But I'm freezing here. |
| OM: | [*Off-stage.*] It's also so cold here... It doesn't differ from out there either. |
| LD: | Come out... Who are you that settled down in my house? |
| OM: | [*Appears at one of the windows.*] Who are you? |
| LD: | I'm the owner of this house. |
| OM: | Me too. |
| LD: | Not at all. |
| OM: | I am... |
| LD: | Where have you the pompous come from? |
| OM: | Exactly where have you come from? |
| LD: | Ah, stop it! Why are you picking on me? |
| OM: | [*Laughs.*] You are not in the picture at all. All my life, I've been waiting for the door of this house to be opened. |
| LD: | Really?!... |

| | |
|---|---|
| OM: | Yeah... Now I don't have to climb over the wall anymore. |
| LD: | To enter my house?! Who did you get permission from? |
| OM: | I got permission from nobody. |
| LD: | I'm telling you to come out. |
| OM: | I don't... I'll feel cold there. |
| LD: | But you've already said it's cold there too. |
| OM: | Well... not that much. |
| LD: | What about me? Shall I freeze to death here? |
| OM: | Like me, you'd better go and find somewhere to live. [*Walks away from behind the window and his voice is heard.*] O', I'm so tired and here is a mess. |
| LD: | I'm cold... Let me come in. |
| OM: | [*Appears behind the window again.*] You should have come herebefore me to settle down. |
| LD: | I'm tired... I'm cold. |
| OM: | If I let you in, you will kick me out or kill me. |
| LD: | No... Please... I'll let you stay in the house too. |
| OM: | It's soon now. It's not the right time for you to come in. First, you should pay off your debts. |
| LD: | Which debts? I owe nobody. |
| OM: | You do... You owe yourself. Wait. I'll come down and let you know. |
| LD: | Owe myself?!... But I did nothing wrong. |
| | [*The* OLD MAN *appears in front of the door.*] |
| OM: | I'm worried if you go inside the house... |
| LD: | What shall I do then? |
| OM: | Go in as I say... ok? |
| LD: | Ok. All right... Which debts shall I pay off? |
| OM: | You've committed the greatest sin. |

LD:  Me...?! Do you mean me who have done nothing but give devotion and have served people for which I've even received Certificates of Appreciation...? I've never hurt even a fly...

OM:  You are a murderer..!

LD:  What?! M...mur...murderer? Me... me?

OM:  Yeah... You'll have to kill me if you want to come in the house.

LD:  Kill you?! I won't kill you. I don't know at all how to kill anybody.

OM:  You do. You, in fact, killed me by coming here... unless you want to go away from here.

LD:  No... I'm not a murderer... [*Shouting.*] I killed nobody...

[*One of the windows opens and the* NEIGHBOR, *who was plowing the snow from the path in front of his house, pokes his head out and looks at the* LOCOMOTIVE DRIVER *as if he doesn't know him.*]

NEIGHBOR:  What's up, man. It's late at night. Everybody is asleep.

LD:  H... Hi...!

NEIGHBOR:  What do you want here?

LD:  N...n...nothing. I just want to go home.

NEIGHBOR:  Well, go home. Why are you shouting then?

LD:  By the way, I brought you a snowplow but you'd left.

NEIGHBOR:  Snowplow...?!

LD:  Yeah... You were right. The snowplow was broken. But... but I can buy you a big one tomorrow if you want.

NEIGHBOR:  But I didn't want any snowplow. I have one.

LD:  Right... I know. I saw that you were plowing the snow from the path in front of your house with difficulty.

NEIGHBOR: [*Confused.*] I don't understand what you mean! Are you talking to me?

LD: Yes... But no matter if you've forgotten it. Anyway...

NEIGHBOR: [*While closing the window.*] Yeah... Anyway...

LD: By the way, sir... Excuse me...

NEIGHBOR: What else?

LD: I... I wanted to ask if you live alone.

NEIGHBOR: What?!

LD: Nothing... I mean if you live with your father.

NEIGHBOR: Father?!

LD: An old man who used to look through the windows of all the houses and eat pieces of bread all the time.

NEIGHBOR: What...?!

LD: He is here now.

NEIGHBOR: [*Horrified.*] Where...?

LD: He believes that I've killed him.

NEIGHBOR: [*Pokes his head out a bit further.*] Ki...i...kill... who?

LD: Your father... but don't worry. He is here now. He is ok... He'd settled down in my house by force.

NEIGHBOR: [*Shouting.*] O' man, what the hell do you want from us late at night? Stop talking nonsense.

LD: D...don't worry... I...

NEIGHBOR: My father died many years ago. What can he do in your house?!

LD: S...sorry. I meant no offense...

NEIGHBOR: What are you talking about? He, may God bless his soul, lived an honorable life.

LD: But...

NEIGHBOR: But what? Who the hell are you? Where the hell is your house?

LD: I've already told you... Here it is.

NEIGHBOR: [*Astonished.*] That house?! The same house with a wooden door?

LD: Right. That's it... How come you've forgotten it?

NEIGHBOR: [*Starts guffawing.*] Did you say that house?!

[*While laughing, the* NEIGHBOR *closes the window. The* LOCOMOTIVE DRIVER *hesitates for a second and tries to keep cool.*]

LD: It... it doesn't matter... He may be in trouble in his life... He didn't really mean it... [*Turns to the* OLD MAN.] You were at fault.

OM: Me?!

LD: [*Pauses a second.*] I don't know... I know nothing... I'm not even allowed to enter my own house.

OM: Have you done anything special outside the house that you want to come in?

LD: What else haven't I done? I... I've lived an honest life all my life. I've made many sacrifices just for them all. [*Points his hand at the windows and the audience.*]

OM: Well, why does nobody know you here?

LD: I don't know... I've helped them reach their destination all my life. But now they don't know who I am.

OM: What about you yourself?

LD: Me?!

OM: Yeah... What was your own destination?

LD: My destination?! I just wanted to help them reach their destination. But... but I wasn't aware that I've been helping a bunch of sleeping passengers reach their destination my whole life... But my house.

OM: Here is mine... All my life, I've lived here in darkness lest anybody becomes aware and kicks me out. I didn't dare turn on even one of the lights. If...if I lose here, I'll die.

| | |
|---|---|
| LD: | Well... Well, I can provide you with a room in the house. |
| OM: | No... I'd like to live alone. Here is either mine or yours. |
| LD: | I promise not to bother you. |
| OM: | How can two strangers live together in a house? |
| LD: | Well, one of us... |
| OM: | ...must be killed by the other one. |
| LD: | Do you mean you want to kill me? |
| OM: | No... You've decided to kill me. |
| LD: | How do you know? |
| OM: | Because you are to enter the house. Am I right? |
| LD: | Right... because here is my own house. |
| OM: | Well, you've killed me... |
| LD: | O'! What are you talking about?... I'm afraid. |
| OM: | [*Takes on a desperate appearance. Puts a big morsel of bread in his mouth.*] You'll finally kill me... I mean you have to kill me. [*Hiccups.*] |
| LD: | Was it stuck in your throat? [*Goes toward the house.*] Wait. I'll fetch you some water. |
| OM: | [*Gets up agilely and stops the* LOCOMOTIVE DRIVER *from going.*] Where are you going?! You the trickster! Did you want to deceive me? Go away... Don't close in on my house. |
| LD: | It's my own house. |
| OM: | Pardon me..., I don't get what you meant. [*Punches the* LOCOMOTIVE DRIVER *hard in his chest.*] You're not reliable at all. |
| LD: | [*Tries to push the* OLD MAN *away.*] Get out of my way... This is my house. |
| OM: | [*Takes the broken snowplow.*] I'll show you who is the owner of this house. |

[*The* OLD MAN, *with a stick in his hand, flies at the* LOCOMOTIVE DRIVER *and beats him hard. The* LOCOMOTIVE DRIVER *flops down on the ground, as if dead.*]

OM: Stop getting lippy with me.

[*The* LOCOMOTIVE DRIVER *gets up with difficulty, goes toward his suitcase and picks it up.*]

OM: Hey, what do you have in there?

[*Giving the* OLD MAN *the cold shoulder, the* LOCOMOTIVE DRIVER *moves a few steps away from the house. The* OLD MAN *gets up and aggressively snatches the suitcase from the* LOCOMOTIVE DRIVER's *hand.*]

LD: Give it back to me...

OM: [*Pushes the* LOCOMOTIVE DRIVER *away with his hand.*] Get out of my way, man.

LD: Keep your hands off it... Don't open it.

[*Without giving an answer, the* OLD MAN *opens the suitcase and spreads out all the contents on the ground. Some pieces of clothing and papers are scattered on the ground.*]

LD: Why did you open it?

OM: What do you have in it then?

LD: I... I didn't want anybody to see them but my children.

OM: Come and gather them all now.

[*The* LOCOMOTIVE DRIVER *gathers the clothes and sits in front of the suitcase which is like a gravestone.*]

LD: [*Starts shivering.*] I'm cold...

OM: It's freezing out tonight. It's getting even colder.

[*The* LOCOMOTIVE DRIVER *looks around, agitated.*]

| | |
|---|---|
| OM: | What's up? What are you looking for? |
| LD: | Noth…thi…nothing… |
| OM: | If you're looking for someone, it's of no use. |
| | [*The window of one of the houses darkens.*] |
| LD: | Why… why don't you go home? |
| OM: | First of all, we should clear up the problem. |
| LD: | What are you talking about? Go away. |
| OM: | You will never leave me alone if I go away. You'll finally kick me out one day unless you turn yourself in. |
| LD: | To whom? |
| OM: | To the police. |
| LD: | What shall I tell them? |
| OM: | Go and tell them that you've killed someone. |
| LD: | But… but maybe they don't believe it. |
| OM: | You should talk convincingly. You don't want it on your conscience for the rest of your life, do you? |
| LD: | Now I must be punished if I'm really a murderer. [*Gets up and goes a few steps away from the* OLD MAN.] |
| OM: | Good luck. |
| LD: | [*Stops and turns back to the* OLD MAN.] Gee whiz, … I've really killed you… Right? |
| OM: | Quite clear… Nobody else is here, is there? |
| LD: | Well… I'd better go turn myself in… |
| OM: | I'm waiting to see what you do. |
| LD: | But I still have doubts about it. |
| OM: | About what? |
| LD: | Whether I can prove that I'm a murderer. |
| OM: | You should trust yourself… |
| LD: | Ok… but without your presence, how can I prove |

that I've killed you?

OM: You should rely on yourself... Don't hesitate... Now, go ahead.

LD: [*Moving away from the* OLD MAN] I'll try to... I should manage it.

OM: Do you promise?

LD: I do. Rest assured.

[*The* LOCOMOTIVE DRIVER *goes toward the gate. The* OLD MAN *enters the house. The alley darkens after the* LOCOMOTIVE DRIVER *and the* OLD MAN *leave the stage. The front light of the stage – the opposite side of the stage – turns on except where there's a metal cabin. The* LOCOMOTIVE DRIVER *stands waiting a few meters away in front of the cabin and the* OLD MAN *sits in the cabin, upstage.*]

LD: Hhh...Hi...

OM: Stop beating around the bush... Here is the court...

LD: I know... That's why...

OM: Well, go ahead and confess to your crime.

LD: Ay...e... aye...

OM: You have to confess anyway. Well, the sooner the better... You're absolutely wrong if you think that you can somehow get rid of the court.

LD: I also...

OM: Nobody could so far live through this court. The rule applies to you as well.

LD: [*Happily.*] How nice... That's what matters most to me... Great!

OM: Everybody says so the first time he ends up here. But then...

LD: Trust me. I've already promised the murder victim.

OM: Go on... Confess.

LD: I've killed someone.

| | |
|---|---|
| OM: | Who have you killed? |
| LD: | Who have I killed?! I don't know. He told me that I'd killed him. |
| OM: | Why did you kill him? |
| LD: | Because he'd settled down in my house. |
| OM: | Whew! Whew! |
| LD: | What's happened? |
| OM: | What an evil deed! I can't imagine anything worse. |
| LD: | Worse than what? |
| OM: | That someone kills his guest. |
| LD: | But he didn't let me in my own house. |
| OM: | Really?! How thick are the exterior walls of your house? |
| LD: | 45 cm. |
| OM: | I believe they're better than thin walls. |
| LD: | Never mind! Anybody can hear everything you say inside... Cold flow penetrates inside as well. |
| OM: | Just what I said... The lightweight construction material should be used. |
| LD: | How come?! All of them are truss walls. |
| OM: | Nobody is to blame. You should have built pillars instead. |
| LD: | Anyway, it's built this way. |
| OM: | But I don't like this construction method. |
| LD: | You should solve the problem anyway. |
| OM: | How then? |
| LD: | Well, do you mean I can't prove that I'm a murderer? |
| OM: | It's up to you if you've already collected enough documents. |
| LD: | Documents?! |
| OM: | Yeah, documents. |

| | |
|---|---|
| LD: | Would you accept a witness's testimony as well? |
| OM: | Who is the witness? |
| LD: | The same man I've killed. |
| OM: | So, the witness statement should also be recorded. |
| LD: | But I'm not sure if he would agree to testify. |
| OM: | Then, the court can't reach a final decision. |
| LD: | Please, …sir… Please… What shall I do then? |
| OM: | [*Closes his notebook and gets ready to leave.*] I'm sorry… I can do nothing. |
| LD: | Well, who else can help me out then? |
| OM: | It can't be done this way. The court reaches the final decision based on convincing evidence. |
| LD: | You should trust my word. Just now, I mean right before I came in here, I talked to the murder victim. He also testified that I've killed him. |
| OM: | Has the written and signed statement of the victim been recorded? |
| LD: | I've already told you that… he doesn't agree to testify at the court. |
| OM: | Well, I can do nothing in this regard. |
| LD: | But you can… do something. You see… |
| OM: | Believe me, I'd like very much to help you. But the law doesn't allow me. |
| LD: | What shall I tell him now? I promised him. |
| OM: | It doesn't matter… Anyway, try to get along well with each other. |
| LD: | How come? Impossible… Could you somehow summon him to the court? |
| OM: | Based on what? |
| LD: | What shall I do? |
| OM: | File a complaint against him to let me summon him to the court. |

LD: What shall I write in my complaint?

OM: [*Gives the* LOCOMOTIVE DRIVER *a pencil and a piece of paper.*] Come on... Write it down... Write that... I hereby would like to.... My legal case has been pending because my file isn't yet completed and due to the absence of the murder victim who doesn't agree at all to appear in the court and testify, I'd strongly like to file a complaint against the murder victim. So, I plead with you, the chief judge of the court, to investigate my case by summoning the murder victim to the court. Finished?

LD: Yes...

OM: Sign it.

LD: [*Signs and gives the paper to the* OLD MAN.] Save me, please. Are you sure that you can summon him to the court?

OM: I'll try to.

LD: What if he doesn't come?

OM: We'll render an award verdict.

LD: Would he come then?

OM: I can't promise you at all. But you should wait anyway till the case is thoroughly investigated. [*In a cold and official tone.*] The court session has ended. The accused is released till the file gets completed.

[*The* OLD MAN *leaves the stage quickly. The* LOCOMOTIVE DRIVER *pauses for a second and then passes the gate to enter the alley. The light of the alley turns on and the stage of the court darkens. The* LOCOMOTIVE DRIVER *goes to the house door and starts knocking. After a while, the* OLD MAN *pokes his head out of the window.*]

OM: Have you returned? Wait. I'll come down.

[*The* OLD MAN *comes down a few seconds later and opens the door.*]

| | |
|---|---|
| OM: | What happened?... Did you succeed? |
| LD: | No... To prove the crime, they needed to hear your testimony. |
| OM: | Surely, you couldn't have talked properly. |
| LD: | I could... but the file was incomplete. |
| OM: | I also can do nothing for you. |
| LD: | But you can. |
| OM: | How come? |
| LD: | You can come and testify at the court... Are you ready and willing to come? |
| OM: | No...! |
| LD: | No?!... Why? |
| OM: | I don't leave here at all. You must have tried another way. |
| LD: | I tried that too. |
| OM: | Why didn't you succeed then? |
| LD: | I would if my house didn't have truss walls. |
| OM: | There you go... Do you see that you can handle it without my help? But you yourself didn't want to. |
| LD: | Now then, I'll take you to the court by force. |
| OM: | [*Starts to get aggressive.*] I won't come. |
| LD: | You have to... because I'm going to give the house a thorough cleaning tomorrow. |
| OM: | First, it must be proven that you've killed me. |
| LD: | You have no right to treat me like this. Do you know who I am? |
| OM: | I don't care at all... be anybody you want to be. |
| LD: | But I'm not anybody... Justice has to be served. It must be proven that I've killed you. |
| OM: | Does it really matter to you? |
| LD: | I learnt about it in the court... but I said nothing to the |

judge. If I can't prove that I've killed you, I'll die … I'll freeze to death outside the house… Above all, I'd like to see my family.

OM: None of my business.

LD: I've spent my whole life providing them with a comfortable life.

OM: But there's no family at all. At first, some used to come in here but nobody has shown up around here for years.

LD: What the hell did you do to them?

OM: I did nothing to them. They left here on their own.

LD: Impossible! You must have made them leave.

OM: It was their own fault. I told them to keep the lights off but they didn't listen.

LD: Do you mean just within the few days that I wasn't here?

OM: No… It lasted a few years.

LD: But they were here at home last week.

OM: It's a long while they are not living here.

LD: I saw them myself.

OM: You thought so. Nobody has been here but me.

LD: They were… I talked to them.

OM: You didn't even notice the light of your house decreasing gradually over the passage of time. You've always lived in the locomotive.

LD: All my life, I've helped the sleeping passengers reach their destination…

OM: I couldn't stay in if the house didn't darken.

LD: Do you mean all the lights of my house have always been off?

OM: Yeah… Didn't you know?

LD: You rascal… You've always kept my house in

darkness.

OM:    You should watch your house instead of a metal cabin.

LD:    I'll turn the lights on... Finally, I got rid of that cabin and its monotonous sound. I'll make my family return home. Never...

OM:    Don't get carried away... What's wrong with you? You have no right to enter the house while I'm here, let alone turn on the lights. I've got a few odds and sods over there.

LD:    [*Looks around.*] Are all my acts of devotion returned like this? Hey! I'm the same who helped you reach your destination – all my life. What a pity!

OM:    Pity for what?

LD:    For everything... whatever...

OM:    [*Coughs harshly.*] It was your own life.

LD:    But that night...!

OM:    [*Coughs a few times.*] Which night?

LD:    The same night that the rail had broken up... I...I could save the lives of all the passengers in time.

OM:    Which passengers are you talking about?

LD:    I don't know... Although all of them were asleep then. It was dark but I had to stay up and repair the rail.

[*The sound of a moving and whistling train is heard.*]

OM:    It's too cold.

[*While coughing, the* OLD MAN *enters the house. The light of the alley turns off and the front part of the stage lightens. The* LOCOMOTIVE DRIVER *passes the gate and starts repairing the rail among the metal scraps with some tools eg, wrench, hammer.*]

LD:    My hands have gone numb.

[*In the darkness of the stage, the* OLD MAN *enters*

*and climbs inside the cabin.*]

OM: You must succeed. A train will approach from the opposite site within the next half an hour.

LD: I can't... my hands have gone numb.

OM: Just one screw is left to be done... Hurry up...

LD: I have a numb feeling in my fingers. [*Lifts the sledgehammer into the air and crashes it into the rail a few times. But after crashing a couple of times, he gives a shriek.*] Ouch! I smashed... my fingers.

OM: You've succeeded... You've saved the lives of all the passengers.

[*The sound of a whistling and passing train is heard and slowly replaced by a prolonged applause. Dressed in neat formal clothes, the* OLD MAN *as the Railway Company's manager stands on the metal cabin and the* LOCOMOTIVE DRIVER *with a bandaged hand stands downstage and bows.*]

LD: Thanks a lot... Yours truly... I've only done my duty...

OM: [*Puts up his hand and the applause is gradually quelled.*] In tribute to this great devotion, missing your thumb and index finger, saving hundreds of lives on board from certain death, repairing the rail and avoiding the train wreck and preventing large expenses, enduring the intolerable cold that dark night, staunch efforts and fruitful services, helping the dear passengers reach their destination and driving the train in the heart of night, stopping at different stations, having a permanent smile on your face, wearing neat outfits, combing your hair and washing up, murmuring pleasant songs while driving, cracking watermelon seeds in a melodious tone in a proper time, and in tribute to other countless services done in time, we put this wreath of flowers, made by strong and safe wires, around your neck.

[*The sound of a loud and prolonged applause is heard again. the* LOCOMOTIVE DRIVER *steps forward and the* OLD MAN *puts the wreath around his neck. The* LOCOMOTIVE DRIVER *bows to the audience downstage.*]

LD: You're just flattering me... Thank you... I've only done my duty.

[*The* LOCOMOTIVE DRIVER *removes the wreath of flowers from his neck and passes the gate while walking backward and bowing. The front part of the stage darkens and the valley lightens. The applause is quelled as the* LOCOMOTIVE DRIVER *enters the alley. The* OLD MAN *leaves the house with a loaf of bread in his hand.*]

OM: [*While putting a large morsel of bread in his mouth.*] Who applauded you?

LD: [*Points to the windows.*] All of them... It seems like only yesterday. [*Puts his hand in his pocket and brings out a few sheets of a newspaper eagerly.*] Here you are... Have a look! Then my picture was posted in all newspapers... I've kept all of them... Look!... It's me... How young I look in them!

OM: Is it your picture?

LD: No, this one is me.

OM: Impossible. This one looks like you much more.

LD: No... Look, this one wearing a bright shirt is me.

OM: But this one resembles you much more in appearance.

LD: How come?... I know myself better than you, anyway.

OM: Your appearance doesn't fit him then.

LD: Well, I've already told you... this is a picture of me when I was young.

OM: Seems the photographer wasn't professional. Did you know him?

LD:      No...

OM:     That's it... It would lead here if you don't know your photographer.

LD:      Do I really look that bad in my picture?

OM:     Awful... Just laugh a while.

LD:      Why?

OM:     Let me see if your laughter is like the one in this picture.

LD:      [*Laughs.*] Do you mean like this?

OM:     It didn't work out... Completely different from each other. Laugh again. Open your mouth wider.

LD:      [*Laughs again and opens his mouth wider.*] Did it work out?

OM:     No... You don't resemble a frog at all.

LD:      What?... A frog?

OM:     I would set fire to the photographer if he took a picture of me like this.

LD:      [*Pulls the newspaper out of the* OLD MAN's *hand.*] Give it to me... Whew... How come it looks like a frog?

OM:     Do you think I don't know the difference between a frog and a man?

LD:      But this... Do you mean I used to be a frog before?

OM:     You must have been so.

LD:      Have you ever seen a frog driving a train?

OM:     Well, why does he have a frog-like smile on his face then?

LD:      I've never seen a frog with a smile on its face... especially with such a kind of smile!

OM:     Smile is smile anyway.

LD:      You are right. But the more I think about it, the more I make sure that I didn't use to be a frog then.

OM: How come?

LD: Look... He who is shaking my hand was my boss. How come he shook a frog's hand then?

OM: You are right... People don't shake frogs' hands. So we come to this conclusion that Mr Photographer took it badly.

LD: It's also possible. But it may seem so because the newspaper is old.

OM: Don't put the blame on the newspaper. You look like a frog in this picture.

LD: But which part of my appearance looks like a frog?

OM: Your smile... your hands which are taking that picture frame.

LD: It's not a picture frame. It's a Certificate of Appreciation.

OM: But it looks more like a picture frame.

LD: No... It might have been distorted in the picture. I put it on the shelf, if you've ever noticed... Didn't you notice it? Wait. I'll fetch it for you...

OM: [*Stops the* LOCOMOTIVE DRIVER *from moving.*]

Not necessary at all. I can see well in darkness. I'll fetch it for you if you'd like to have a look.

[*The* OLD MAN *goes toward the house and the* LOCOMOTIVE DRIVER *follows him. The* OLD MAN *stands in front of the door and pushes the* LOCOMOTIVE DRIVER *away.*]

OM: Move back.

LD: Let me come in.

OM: How? It's not proven yet that you killed me.

LD: I promise you I'll come out.

OM: No... You can see nothing inside there.

LD: Well, I'll turn on the light.

OM: No... If just a weak ray of light leaks from the window

I can't stay in the house anymore. I've never turned on a light in the house all my life. Now, move back.

[*The* OLD MAN *enters the house and closes the door behind him. Another window of the* NEIGH-BOR's *house darkens. The* OLD MAN *pokes his head out of the window and shows a picture frame.*]

OM: Do you mean this one?

LD: That's it...

OM: [*Holds the picture frame out of the window.*] Here you go... Take it.

LD: [*Takes the frame.*] O'..., nothing is here! [*Drops the frame on the ground, horrified. Opens his suitcase, looks at some papers and cardboard inside a file, and begins shouting.*] All of them are false... What is true then?

OM: Get out of here...

LD: I don't... The only place left for me is my house. [*Tears up the Certificates of Appreciations and newspapers angrily and hastily.*] All of them are false...

OM: Don't tear them up.

LD: Get lost... Although I kept on going, I've been led nowhere. I was confined to that metal cabin and my eyes followed the infinite sequence of the timbers used to tie two parallel rails that never meet each other.

OM: But one of those rails broke up once and you repaired it and tied them again. Have you forgotten?

LD: No... I remember it and you as well... You were right... I looked like a frog croaking in a frozen marsh... where I mistakenly thought as the whole world. You outsmarted me and forced your way into my house... Now I've returned. I can no more stand cold weather and wandering out there.

OM: [*Greedily puts a few morsels of bread in his mouth.*]

I won't come out.

LD:     I myself will kick you out.

[*The* LOCOMOTIVE DRIVER *makes a sudden rush toward the window. But the* OLD MAN *punches him out to keep him away the window.*]

OM:     Stay away… Don't get close to me…

LD:     Come out… [*He enters the house while being beaten by the* OLD MAN.]

OM:     Don't come in…

[*Their shouting and the clanks of the stuff is heard from inside the house.*]

OM:     [*Off-stage.*] No… Let it go.

LD:     [*Off-stage.*] Go away… damn you. Here should be cleaned.

[*Some pieces of trash including torn papers, railroad ties, and empty cans are thrown out of the window. Then a weak ray of light leaks from the window.*]

LD:     [*Off-stage.*] Jerk…! You've gathered garbage in my house for a long while.

OM:     [*Off-stage.*] This is my stuff.

LD:     [*Off-stage.*] Stay away… Get lost…

OM:     [*Off-stage, with his mouth full.*] No… Give it to me…

[*A full sack is thrown out of the window. The light, which is leaking from the window, widens.*]

LD:     [*Off-stage.*] I must throw away all the stuff here.

[*Another full sack and some other pieces of torn papers and metal scraps are thrown out of the window. The light, which is leaking from the window, widens much more.*]

LD:     [*Off-stage.*] Here should be as clean as the first day.

[*Again other garbage including a broken chair and table are thrown out of the window. The window brightens even more, till it lightens the alley completely.*]

OM:    [*Off-stage.*] You killed me by doing this.

LD:    [*Off-stage.*] You don't belong here anymore... Get lost...

[*The house door opens and the* OLD MAN *is thrown out of the house. The door is closed quickly. The* OLD MAN *bursts out laughing morbidly and hastily puts large morsels in his mouth. Drowned in the room's light, the* LOCOMOTIVE DRIVER *appears at the window.*]

OM:    [*Still laughing.*] I lied... I never die... Now I'm going to another house... There are so many houses in this town...

*The* OLD MAN *goes toward the thrown-out garbage and after taking some, goes toward one of the other houses and enters it cautiously and quickly.*

*The lights dim.*

www.ingramcontent.com/pod-product-compliance
Lightning Source LLC
Chambersburg PA
CBHW071813200626
46813CB00020B/2261